THE ICE ARENA

THE BUBBLE GUM VOLCANO

THE CITY OF BUTTERFLIES

THE SEA FOREST

THE SLEEPING WHALE

THE PAPER MOUNTAINS

THE SWEET SEA ISLANDS

THE CAPE OF FLYING FISH

© Ana de Lima illustrated these marvelous oddities just as she had imagined them in her mind.
© Mia Cassany wrote about these places just as she had pictured them in her dreams.
One day, both of them sat down together for some coffee and carrot cake. They talked about maps and
came up with colors and languages for an atlas that would never exist like this. Or would it?

© for the Spanish edition: 2016, Mosquito Books, Barcelona,
SL Ramón y Cajal 44 - 08012 Barcelona (Spain)
www.mosquitobooksbarcelona.com
Title of the original edition: Atlas de los lugares que no existen
© for text and illustrations: 2016, Ana de Lima
© for the English edition: 2018, 3rd printing 2020, Prestel Verlag, Munich · London · New York
A member of Verlagsgruppe Random House GmbH
Neumarkter Strasse 28 · 81673 Munich

Prestel Publishing Ltd.
14-17 Wells Street
London W1T 3PD

Prestel Publishing
900 Broadway, Suite 603
New York, NY 10003

Library of Congress Control Number: 2017953133
A CIP catalogue record for this book is available from the British Library.

Translation: Paul Kelly
Copyediting: Brad Finger
Production management: Astrid Wedemeyer
Typesetting: textum Gmbh, Feldafing
Printing and binding: TBB, a.s.
Paper: Tauro

Verlagsgruppe Random House FSC® N001967

Printed in Slovakia
ISBN 978-3-7913-7347-8
www.prestel.com

An Atlas
of Imaginary Places

Mia Cassany * Ana de Lima

Prestel
Munich · London · New York

Every night I dream of a magical place – a place
that only exists in my mind for a brief moment.
You can explore this make-believe world in the
atlas. In my imagination, however, it really exists.

I fantasize and journey through a world in which
the impossible is normal and the possible is
jumbled up. Come with me, give me your hand
and let's take a peek at a world that only becomes
visible when we dream together.

Come with me to places that will surprise
and inspire you.

Atchoo!
Every time someone sneezes,
the animals change their
coats. If at first they were silky
soft with black and white
stripes, they later become
wiry and spotted the next time
you sneeze. You cannot
remember what they
looked like at first
because as soon as
you sneeze...

In this enchanted sea lives the most beautiful
of lady giants. She folds together small paper
boats and fills them with sweet aromas. Then she
gently lets the boats drift out into the water...

When the sweet-scented boats slowly fill up with water and sink into the sea, small, oddly-shaped islands begin to form. Locals call this place the Sweet Sea Islands.

In the neighboring bay there lives a sleeping whale. Is he always asleep? Yes ... and he will never wake up until all the city's inhabitants fall into a deep sleep on his back at the same time. Don't worry, however, because this will never happen. No city is ever completely asleep!

And so, the good whale snores peacefully in his shelter. Protected from the waves, he doesn't even notice that each of his loud snores causes heaps of fish to rain down on the city.

Here you can look stars and planets right in the eye from the fantasy world's tallest lighthouse. If you dare to climb all the way up, you can use your finger to draw a new galaxy.

Let's think up some music! Beautiful
sounds echo far over the ice.
Each afternoon, pole dwellers gather
to enjoy the world's coolest rhythms.

Welcome to the mountains that grow upside down. It's even possible to swing between them! Should you fall, there will be a host of soft clouds waiting to catch you.

What kind of weird creatures grow in this forest? The giant waves created by the winter wind have washed countless sea creatures into the trees. Winter has raged so hard that, over time, these animals have learned to live in trees.

A huge volcano is not always as terrifying as you might think. Because each time this volcano erupts, it spits out lava made from bubble gum in every imaginable color and flavor! All the bubble gum in the world comes from this fantasy volcano.

The inhabitants of this big city once heard that they should talk and sing to the plants. And that's exactly what they did. But what happened afterwards? The lavish sprouting plants decided to move into the city's streets and buildings. Today, this place is called the Lush Green City.

The other big metropolis in this make-believe world is the City of Butterflies. When the city's people are sad or worried, they simply look upwards and marvel at the variety of colorful winged creatures protecting them.

In a land where nothing is impossible, the real is unreal and everything is upside down. Here you can find a hidden lake with crystal clear water. Hundreds of different fruits and vegetables grow there. They ripen amongst the swans, fish and algae.

Did you know there was a place where everything we always seem to lose is collected? It's the Desert of Lost and Found, of course! When the wind blows and the sand covers a misplaced object, it flies back into some random house. How fortunate would it be if you were to lose your glasses, but ended up finding a shoe in your living room instead!

In the universe of fantastic places, it's easy to lose your way.
Only those who do not get lost in the Labyrinth of Dreams
make it to the summit and live under the clear blue sky.
There they can wish for anything they want.

THE TALLEST LIGHTHOUSE

THE LUSH GREEN CITY

THE HIDDEN LAKE

THE LABYRINTH OF DESIRES

THE UPSIDE-DOWN MOUNTAINS

THE JUNGLE OF CHANGING SPOTS

THE DESERT OF LOST AND FOUND

N
O E
S